I AM READING

Granddad's Dinosaur

BROUGH GIRLING

ILLUSTRATED BY
STEPHEN DELL

KINGFISHER
BOSTON

KINGFISHER
a Houghton Mifflin Company imprint
222 Berkeley Street
Boston, Massachusetts 02116
www.houghtonmifflinbooks.com

First published by Kingfisher in 1997
This edition published in 2005
2 4 6 8 10 9 7 5 3 1
1TR/0904/AJT/ – (SACH)115MA/F

LIBRARY OF CONGRESS CATALOGING-IN-PUBLICATION DATA
has been applied for.

ISBN 0-7534-5897-7
ISBN 978-07534-5897-6

Printed in India

Contents

Chapter One

This is Sally.

And this is
Sally's granddad.

Sally's granddad has a big, cluttered
backyard with a pond.

Granddad said Sally could try to catch
some tadpoles in the pond.
So Sally went to the garage
to get a fishnet.

Sally's granddad

has a messy garage.

Sally couldn't find a fishnet anywhere.

She looked under some boxes . . .

She looked on a shelf . . .

She looked in a cupboard . . .

but there was no fishnet.

Then Sally heard a rustling noise.

It was coming from behind

a pile of old magazines . . .

Suddenly,

out jumped the strangest creature

Sally had ever seen.

It was bright red

and around the size of a large dog.

Sally was amazed.

"Hello there!" said the creature.

Sally was even more amazed.

"You must be Sally!

I've heard your granddad

talking about you."

Sally looked frightened.

"Don't be scared,"

said the creature.

"I'm only

a dinosaur!"

"A dinosaur!" said Sally.

"Oh, I know people think that

dinosaurs are great big creatures

with long tails and tall necks,"

the dinosaur went on.

"And everyone thinks

we died out years ago.

But there are still a few of us little

ones around.

It's just that humans don't often spot us.

You have to be very quick

and very lucky

to see a dinosaur."

And he smiled at Sally.

Come on, let's get going!"

And he handed Granddad's best fishnet

to Sally.

Chapter Two

Sally and the small red dinosaur
started to walk through the yard.
Suddenly, the dinosaur spotted
Granddad's clothesline.
It was covered in clothes
that Granddad had washed
that morning.
"Hey!" said the dinosaur.
"Look at that!
I just love those crazy things!"

"What things?" said Sally.

"Those crazy

wishy-washy-whirly-giggy things!

Have you ever had a spin on one?"

"What do you mean?" asked Sally.

"I'll show you!" grinned the dinosaur.

Before Sally knew what was happening,

the dinosaur leaped onto

Granddad's clothesline

and started to spin around and around.

"WHEEEEEE!!!

Watch me go!"

Soon the clothes

started flying off the line.

A striped towel went first,

then a pair of swim trunks

and one of Granddad's old vests.

Sally started to laugh.

19

Then she heard the creak
of a window opening!
In a flash,
the dinosaur dropped
to the ground
and hid behind
a pot of flowers.

"Sally!" called Granddad.

"My whiskers!

The wind has started to blow a little,

hasn't it?

Put those clothes back on the line,

there's a good girl."

And Granddad shut the window

with a bang.

Sally started to pick up the clothes.

"Do you think he saw us?"

asked the dinosaur

from behind the flowers.

"I don't think so," said Sally.

Chapter Three

Sally and the small red dinosaur
started to walk to the pond.

"Hey! Look at that!"
said the dinosaur suddenly.

23

"There's one of those fabulous
off-you-go-scooters!
I love them!"
The dinosaur was pointing
to a small wagon.
Sally's granddad used it
to move his garbage
can from the back
door to the yard.
"Have you ever
had a ride on one?"
asked the dinosaur.
"Quick! Jump on!"
Before Sally knew what was happening,
the dinosaur was on the wagon.

Sally got on behind him.

The dinosaur scooted the wagon along

with one back leg.

He steered with his front paws.

"WHEEEE!!!" shouted the dinosaur.

They went very fast along the path.

"How do we stop?" cried Sally.

"Easy!" said the dinosaur.

26

The next moment they crashed

SLAP!

BANG!

right into

Granddad's garbage can!

The wagon,

Sally,

and the small red dinosaur

flew through the air . . .

and landed in the cabbage patch.

The lid of the garbage can
fell on the ground
with a huge BANG!
It sounded like an elephant
walking into a pair of cymbals.

Then Sally heard
the creak of a window opening.

29

"Sally!" called Granddad.

"My whiskers! Now the wind has

blown off the garbage can lid!

Put it back for me,

there's a good girl."

"Yes, Granddad," said Sally.

"Do you think he saw us?"

whispered the dinosaur.

"I don't think so," said Sally.

Chapter Four

Sally and the small red dinosaur
saw the garden hose and sprinkler
lying on the lawn.

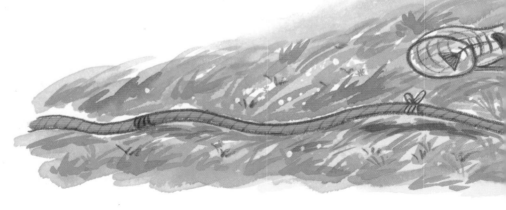

"Hey! Look at that!" cried the dinosaur.
"A sprinkly-winkly-roundy-wetter!
Great! Turn the water on, Sally,
and watch me go!"

Sally turned it on and waited.

Then the dinosaur did an amazing thing.

As the sprinkler started to turn around,

he stood in the middle of it.

Then he began to do all kinds

of clever tricks.

As the sprinkler
went faster,
the dinosaur
balanced on
one leg.

He did a
handstand.

He even stood
on his head.

"WHOOOOOOSH!!!
Speed it up, Sally!
This is fantastic!"

Sally turned the water on full
blast and went to join in the fun.
She ran around and around
the spinning dinosaur
until she began to feel
very dizzy.
The water splashed everywhere,
and they both got very wet!

"You're fantastic too!" giggled Sally.
"I didn't know dinosaurs could be like you!"

The dinosaur went faster

and faster

and faster!

Then he began to wobble.

Just when he was trying

a very difficult tail stand,

the sprinkler tipped over.

A jet of water

sprayed into Sally's face.

As Sally tried to get out of the way,

her feet got mixed up

with the dinosaur's feet.

They both tripped over the hose—

and each other.

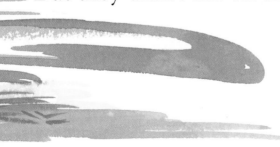

But they didn't fall on the wet lawn . . .

they fell into Granddad's pond!

Then they heard

the creak of a window opening.

"Sally!" called Granddad.

"My whiskers!

Now it's started to rain.

You'd better come in,

there's a good girl."

"Yes, Granddad," said Sally,

still sitting in the cold, muddy water.

"Do you think he saw us?"

asked the dinosaur.

"I don't think so," said Sally

as she got out of the pond

and dripped back toward the house.

Chapter Five

Later that evening

Sally and Granddad were reading

a book together.

The book was called

The Wonderful World of Dinosaurs.

There were lots of pictures
of great big dinosaurs
with long tails and tall necks.

Suddenly, Sally spotted
a *small* dinosaur.
It was red.
It looked *exactly* like the dinosaur
in Granddad's garage.
"Hey, look at that!" cried Sally.
"My whiskers!" said Granddad.

"I didn't know

there were any *red* dinosaurs!

This one was called a

DO-YOU-THINK-HE-SAURUS.

The book says sometimes people are still

lucky enough to see one!

But I don't believe that, do you, Sally?"

Sally started to giggle . . .

and so did somebody else!

About the author and illustrator

Brough Girling has written many books for children. He lives in Oxfordshire, England, where he and his wife raise some sheep, chickens, ducks, and a cow. "But sadly," says Brough, "we don't have any red dinosaurs . . . at least we've never seen one!"

Stephen Dell worked in advertising for many years, but *Granddad's Dinosaur* was his first book. He says, "I really enjoyed drawing the little dinosaur getting up to so much mischief—I wish I'd met a dinosaur when I was younger!" Stephen lives in London, England, with his wife and daughter.

Strategies for Independent Readers

Predict
Think about the cover, illustrations, and the title of the book. What do you think this book will be about? While you are reading think about what may happen next and why.

Monitor
As you read ask yourself if what you're reading makes sense. If it doesn't, reread, look at the illustrations, or read ahead.

Question
Ask yourself questions about important ideas in the story such as what the characters might do or what you might learn.

Phonics
If there is a word that you do not know, look carefully at the letters, sounds, and word parts that you do know. Blend the sounds to read the word. Ask yourself if this is a word you know. Does it make sense in the sentence?

Summarize
Think about the characters, the setting where the story takes place, and the problem the characters faced in the story. Tell the important ideas in the beginning, middle, and end of the story.

Evaluate
Ask yourself questions like: Did you like the story? Why or why not? How did the author make the story come alive? How did the author make the story fun to read? How well did you understand the story? Maybe you can understand it better if you read it again!